THIS WALKER BOOK BELONGS TO:

_____

_____   _____

_____   _____

_____   _____

FOR
SEBASTIAN WALKER
WHO STIRRED it all up
FOR THE Best.

First published 1993 by Walker Books Ltd
87 Vauxhall Walk, London SE11 5HJ

This edition published 1995

2 4 6 8 10 9 7 5 3

© 1993 by John Burningham

Printed in Hong Kong

This book has been typeset in Galliard.

British Library Cataloguing in Publication Data
A catalogue record for this book
is available from the British Library.

ISBN 0-7445-4323-1

Harvey Slumfenburger's Christmas Present

John Burningham

WALKER BOOKS
AND SUBSIDIARIES
LONDON • BOSTON • SYDNEY

It was Christmas Eve.
Father Christmas and the
reindeer were home at last.
They were very tired, because
they had been delivering presents
to all the children everywhere.

They had something to eat, then Father Christmas put the reindeer to bed. One of the reindeer said it did not feel very well, perhaps it had nibbled something on the way that it should not have.

Father Christmas thought
that all it needed was a
good night's sleep.

Finally Father Christmas was able to go to bed. He put on his pyjamas and was just climbing into bed when he saw something that made him gasp. At the end of his bed lay his sack. Father Christmas could see the shape of one present still inside it.

Father Christmas pulled the present out of the sack. The present was Harvey Slumfenburger's.

Father Christmas knew all about Harvey Slumfenburger. He knew that Harvey Slumfenburger's parents were too poor to buy him presents. He knew that Harvey Slumfenburger only ever got one present, and that was the present which Father Christmas brought him. He knew that Harvey Slumfenburger lived in a hut at the top of the Roly Poly Mountain, which was far, far away.

Father Christmas was very tired.
The reindeer were asleep and one of them was
not very well. But Father Christmas knew he
had to get the present to Harvey Slumfenburger.

Father Christmas put on his coat over his pyjamas.
He put on his boots and hat, picked up the sack with
Harvey Slumfenburger's present in it, and started

to walk through the cold winter night to the hut
where Harvey Slumfenburger lived at the top of
the Roly Poly Mountain, which was far, far away.

Father Christmas had not gone very far when
he met a man with an aeroplane. "Excuse me,"
he said, "my name is Father Christmas. I still have
one present left in my sack, which is for Harvey
Slumfenburger, the little boy who lives in a hut
at the top of the Roly Poly Mountain, which is far,
far away. And it will soon be Christmas Day."
  "Get in my plane," said the man, "and I will
take you as far as I can." The aeroplane took
off and flew through the night sky towards
the Roly Poly Mountain.

Heavy snow began to fall.

"I am so sorry, Father Christmas," said the man. "I cannot fly my aeroplane any further in this snow." The plane bumped and skidded across the ground and finally came to a halt. "But if you go to the garage that lies over the hill, there is a man with a Jeep. Perhaps he can help you."

Father Christmas set off through the snow.
He went over the hill to the garage where there
was the man with the Jeep. "Excuse me," he said,
"my name is Father Christmas. I still have one
present left in my sack, which is for Harvey
Slumfenburger, the little boy who lives in a hut
at the top of the Roly Poly Mountain, which is
far, far away. And it will soon be Christmas Day."
  "Climb in my Jeep," said the man, "and I will
take you as far as I can."
    The Jeep bounced and spun across the fields and
down the road towards the Roly Poly Mountain.

But then the Jeep skidded and crashed through
the fence and into a tree. Father Christmas was sent
tumbling into the snow.

"I am so sorry, Father Christmas," said the man.
"I can take you no further. But if you go down
the hill and across the river there is a boy
with a motorbike. Perhaps
the boy can help you."

Father Christmas went down the hill and across the river and met the boy with the motorbike. "Excuse me," he said, "my name is Father Christmas. I still have one present left in my sack, which is for Harvey Slumfenburger, the little boy who lives in a hut at the top of the Roly Poly Mountain, which is far, far away. And it will soon be Christmas Day."

 "We'll go on my motorbike," said the boy. "I will take you as far as I can."

The motorbike roared off along the road towards the Roly Poly Mountain.

But they had not gone very far before the
motorbike slid on some ice and they both fell off.
"I am so sorry, Father Christmas," said the boy.
"The front of my bike is all twisted and I can take
you no further. But if you go across the valley and
into the woods there is a girl who has skis.
Perhaps she can help you."

Father Christmas went across the valley and into the woods, where he found the girl with skis. "Excuse me," he said, "my name is Father Christmas. I still have one present left in my sack, which is for Harvey Slumfenburger, the little boy who lives in a hut at the top of the Roly Poly Mountain, which is far, far away. And it will soon be Christmas Day."

"Stand on the back of my skis," said the girl, "and I will take you as far as I can towards the Roly Poly Mountain."

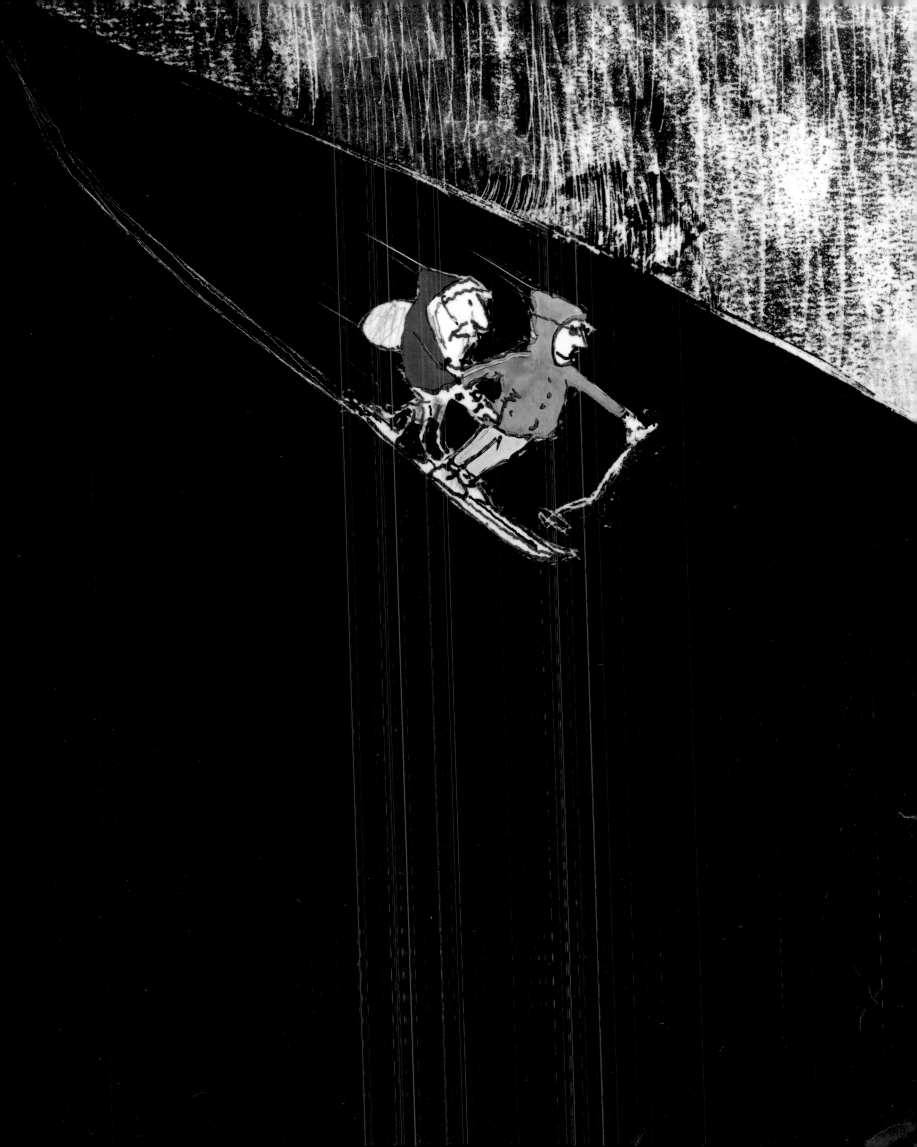

They had not gone very far when the skis broke
with a crack and they both tumbled into the snow.

"I am so sorry, Father Christmas," said the girl.
"My skis are broken and I can take you no further.
But if you go up the slope and down onto
the plain you will be near the bottom of the
Roly Poly Mountain, where there
is a climber with a rope.
Perhaps he can help you."

Father Christmas went up the slope and down onto the plain, where he found the climber with the rope. "Excuse me," he said, "my name is Father Christmas. I still have one present left in my sack, which is for Harvey Slumfenburger, the little boy who lives in a hut at the top of the Roly Poly Mountain, which is far, far away. And it will soon be Christmas Day."

"Hold on to my rope," said the climber, "and I will take you as far as I can up the Roly Poly Mountain."

They had not climbed very far when
the rope broke and Father Christmas
nearly fell off the Roly Poly Mountain.
"I am so sorry, Father Christmas,"
said the climber. "My rope is broken
and I cannot climb any higher. But if
you carry on up that cliff and over
those boulders you will see a little hut
at the top, and that is the hut where
Harvey Slumfenburger lives."

Father Christmas carried on up the cliff and over the boulders and finally arrived at the hut where Harvey Slumfenburger lived.

Father Christmas
climbed onto
the roof and
down the
chimney…

and put the present in Harvey Slumfenburger's stocking.

Then Father Christmas
set off on the long
journey home.

Father Christmas
checked that the
reindeer were
all right and tucked
up in bed.

And as the sun began to rise on Christmas
morning, Father Christmas climbed into bed
and was soon fast asleep.

In the hut at the top of the Roly Poly Mountain, which is far, far away, a little boy, whose name was Harvey Slumfenburger, reached for the stocking on the end of his bed and took out his present.

I wonder what it was.

MORE WALKER PAPERBACKS
For You to Enjoy

FIRST STEPS
by John Burningham

"Colours, opposites, numbers, letters – first concepts are great fun to discover in this delightful book." *Parents*

0-7445-4320-7   £4.99

FARMER DUCK
by Martin Waddell/Helen Oxenbury

Winner of the Smarties Book Prize and
Highly Commended for the Kate Greenaway Medal

"Marvellously expressive pictures and a satisfying text make this the outstanding picture book of the year." *The Sunday Times*

0-7445-3660-X   £4.50

KING OF KINGS
by Susan Hill/John Lawrence

A lonely old man discovers an abandoned baby in this moving, modern-day, urban nativity story.

"Heartwarming in the way that Christmas stories ought to be." *The Times*

0-7445-4326-6   £4.50